Making Reading Fun!

Chrysalis Children's Books

In memory of Mum
S. H.

Author's note

I first came up with the idea for *The Lady Who Lived in a Car* after reading an article in the newspaper about
the real 'Miss Lettuce', Miss Anne Smith, whose home for thirty years was an old Ford Consul in a London
suburb. Over the months my story, though partly based on the real lady, has taken on its own life.
In my interpretation, all of the characters are fictitious, though some perhaps are influenced by people I know!
Inspired by the struggle of this lady to remain a resident in the neighbourhood where she had grown up,
I hope *The Lady Who Lived in a Car* shows us that sometimes our differences can be a good thing.

First published in Great Britain in 2004 by
Chrysalis Children's Books
an imprint of Chrysalis Books Group plc
The Chrysalis Building, Bramley Road, London, W10 6SP
www.chrysalisbooks.co.uk
This paperback edition first published in 2005

Designed by Sarah Goodwin and Keren-Orr Greenfeld

A CIP catalogue record for this book is available
from the British Library.

ISBN 1 84365 028 2 (hardback)
ISBN 1 84458 055 5 (paperback)

Set in Lady Car
Printed in China

2 4 6 8 10 9 7 5 3 1

This book can be ordered direct from the publisher. Please contact
the Marketing Department. But try your bookshop first.

The Lady
Who Lived
In A Car

Suzanna
Hubbard

Chrysalis Children's Books

My name is Molly. Me and my brother, Charlie, live in Robinson Street. It's nothing special. Quite ordinary really, well, except for Miss Lettuce who lives in a car.

Miss Lettuce can tame the local wildlife ...

and Miss Lettuce can ride on a unicycle
with Smiler her dog on her head ...

and Miss Lettuce can play on the big bass drum ...

and Miss Lettuce tells us ...

...the best stories EVER!

She tells us about her days spent in the circus, and about the time when Smiler jumped through the hoop and landed on a bald man's head.

She tells us about her travels as a dancer on the big ships and of how she met a handsome captain and -oh!- how they fell in love!

But now Miss Lettuce lives in a car, she says, "I wouldn't change it for all the Lapsang Souchong tea in China."
And in the boot of her car she keeps the most amazing collection of hats to suit all her moods.

Jolly

Shy

Silly

Grumpy

But there is one man on the street who doesn't like hats:
Mr Brushwood. He doesn't like ...

silly hats or peculiar cats, dirty rats, flapping bats, little dogs, noisy clogs, slimy frogs

worms in jars, Spanish guitars and especially ladies who live in cars!

One day Mr Brushwood wrote a letter to everybody in Robinson Street and this is what it said: "It's time Miss Lettuce got herself a proper home."

Mr H.Brushwood
62 Robinson Street
Wigmouth
WW1 3AB

Dear Resident,

I am writing to you concerning Miss Lettuce and her car. Miss Lettuce has lived in her car for many years and quite frankly I feel it has seen better days.

I hope you will agree with me in saying that IT'S TIME MISS LETTUCE GOT HERSELF A PROPER HOME (the sort that normal people live in).

Yours sincerely,

Horace Brushwood

H.Brushwood

Me and Charlie took the letter straight to Miss Lettuce.

"What shall we do?" we said.

Miss Lettuce put on her thinking cap, a feathery owl-shaped hat.

I know!

"I know!" she said. "I will challenge Mr Brushwood to a contest.
If he wins, then I will leave Robinson Street. But if I win,
he must wear one of my hats."

So we knocked at Mr Brushwood's door and told him our plan for a big competition. "Will you say yes?" we asked.

And with a fat grin and a sly look in his eye he said, "Yes, I'll do it."

First we had a hula-hoop competition. Hooray! Miss Lettuce came first with one hundred and forty-eight (and a half) hoops.

Second up was the enormous jam-tart-eating competition, but ... oh dear ... Mr Brushwood gobbled his jam tart down in one!

Next we had the can-can dancing competition. Yippee! Miss Lettuce won again, with a hundred and sixty-five kicks.

Then we had the pea-soup-drinking competition. Would you believe it? Mr Brushwood drank all his soup and Miss Lettuce's in one go.

And if that wasn't enough to make you feel sick, last of all we had a skipping-in-frog-suits competition. Miss Lettuce and Mr Brushwood skipped up and down Robinson Street.

They skipped ... and they skipped ...

and they skipped ... until finally ...

Mr Brushwood was sick everywhere! Pea soup and jam tart...

Poor Mr Brushwood felt very ill ...

But at least Miss Lettuce gave him
her get-well-soon hat to wear ...

And thank goodness Miss Lettuce is here to stay.

More fun books for you to read!

Lewis Carroll
Illustrated by
Michael Foreman

ISBN 1 84365 056 8

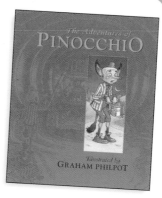

The Adventures of
PINOCCHIO

Illustrated by
GRAHAM PHILPOT

ISBN 1 84458 140 3 (pb)

ebby meets
Felicity

Matt Hickey
Illustrated by
Christopher Corr

ISBN 1 84365 061 4

ARCHIE'S
AMAZING
ADVENTURE

SALLY GRINDLEY
ILLUSTRATED BY
JOHN BENDALL-BRUNELLO

ISBN 1 84365 026 6 (hb)
ISBN 1 84458 157 8 (pb)

Princess
Stories
From Around the World

Retold by Kate Tym
Illustrated by Sophy Williams

ISBN 1 84365 025 8

GIANT
TALES

RETOLD BY FIONA WATERS
ILLUSTRATED BY AMANDA HALL

ISBN 1 84365 017 7